The Story of a Troll-Hunt

The Story of a Troll-Hunt

Written and Drawn
by

James McBryde

Coachwhip Publications
Landisville, Pennsylvania

The Story of a Troll-Hunt
Written and drawn by James McBryde (1874-1904)
Introduction by M. R. James (1862-1936)

ISBN 1-930585-25-X

Published by Coachwhip Publications. 2006.

Originally published (in limited edition) 1904 by Cambridge University Press as a memorial tribute to James McBryde.

Coachwhipbooks.com

Contents

Introduction, by M. R. James 7

The Story of a Troll-Hunt 11

Translation of Script 91

Introduction

The issuing of these pictures affords an opportunity—which comes also in the aspect of a duty—of writing a few prefatory lines about him who drew them. Welcome as it is, I do not think any task could be more difficult; and I ask forgiveness beforehand, if by chance I strike a jarring note. For incompleteness the reader must be prepared; these few pages make no pretence of containing a connected biographical sketch.

I speak as one who first came to know James McBryde when he entered at Cambridge eleven years ago, and who, ever since our first meeting, have found in his friendship an unfailing source of content. No one whom I have known could enlist the warmest affection more easily or retain it more surely. There was no companion who so completed a circle,—no one who, even when he supposed himself to be out of spirits, brought so much enjoyment into an expedition. A smile will never be fair off when his friends speak of him.

All this was obvious, and on the surface. At the same time I do not believe that anyone could have thought him shallow. The determination with which he accomplished his medical course, a great deal of which was at the time entirely against the grain (his progress, we shall all remember was marked throughout by loud and picturesque complaints) was enough to refute any such notion. How helpful he was in a difficulty, how unselfish and considerate always, would be realized very quickly: the depths of his affection, and the strength of his loyalty, few can have fully sounded and tested.

For a great part of his life the stress of his work kept him away from literature, and I can remember the time when a single novel of ordinary dimensions would last him through a whole summer. That, I must say, was in quite early days: as time went on, he developed a very sure taste in the matter of books, just as he did in the matter of drawing, and of art in general.

Pictorial art was, after all, his great pleasure and interest. It is idle to speculate on what he might have achieved in a long life: what I know is that the work he has left, whether it is conceived in a serious or in a humorous spirit, have qualities that never fail to attract, and always abide in the memory. Closely bound up in our minds with his drawings is his talk. His descriptions of his experiences were a perpetual delight: they were coloured by that humour and that brilliant faculty of observation which were part of him, and by a vocabulary that was all his own: they never failed nor palled.

Among lesser ingredients that lent a savour to the manner and matter of his narratives were an admirable tortuousness of expression—which defies reproduction—and an astonishing aptitude for encountering small misadventures. "This has been a bad day," he writes, "I began by missing three trains at three different changes, walked two miles in the rain, missed my train back, then caught another which took me to the wrong place, and have just spilt the entire ink-pot all over my cloth." But these occurrences, which would have reduced most of us to sulky rage, left his serenity unimpaired.

For the accident (he always described it as an accident) which enabled him to pass into King's, the College may be very grateful. The presence in it of so much affection, truth, innocence, and humour could not but make an enormous difference to the atmosphere of the place; and how much pleasure of the best kind his companionship brought into the lives of his nearer friends it is not possible for one of them, at least, to put into words.

He was at once so transparently and simply good, and so strong in varied capabilities and interests, that I cannot hope to bring out all the aspects of him upon which his friends might wish me to dwell, within the limits which I regard as fitting: and, after many efforts to fill in the picture, I have come to think that the wisest course will be to leave it as a faint sketch. But it is with reluctance that I renounce the effort, and I hope that the renunciation may be only temporary.

As Time one day by me did pass;
  Through a large dusky glasse
  He held, I chanc'd to look,
  And spyed his curious Book
Of past days, where sad Heav'n did shed
A mourning light upon the dead.

Many disordered lives I saw,
  And foul records, which thaw
  My kinde eyes still; but in
  A fair white page of thin
And ev'n, smooth lines, like the sun's rays,
Thy name was writ, and all thy days.

O bright and happy kalendar!
  Where youth shines like a star
  All pearl'd with tears, and may
  Teach age the Holy way;
Where through thick pangs, high agonies,
Faith into life breaks, and death dies. [1]

The intercourse of eleven years,—of late minutely recalled,—has left no single act or word of his which I could wish to forget.

The sheets reproduced in this book were written and drawn at various times in 1899 and 1900. They were the outcome of an expedition to Denmark which I made with James McBryde and W. J. Stone in the August of 1899. Will Stone was our companion again in Denmark and Sweden in 1900; and in February, 1901, he died. There is much that I could say in remembrance of him also: but that work is reserved for other hands.

The three travellers who appear in the pictures may be taken to represent us three; not,—one is permitted to hope,—with photographic accuracy. The idea of the Troll-hunt was perhaps suggested by myself. It was eagerly adopted, because we had all been much engrossed by the folklore of Jutland, which peoples its wide and lonely heaths with many strange beings. The working-out is entirely due to McBryde, and gives as characteristic a specimen of his particular humour, both in the pictures and in the text, as it is now possible to procure.

I think it not out of place to inscribe this book to the memory of my two fellow-travellers;

"now no longer sojourners, but citizens."

M. R. J.

November, 1904.

[1] These lines are by Henry Vaughan.

The Story of a Troll-Hunt

One Evening, while discussing our plans for the Long Vac.

the idea occurred to us three of making an Expedition to Denmark with the object of bringing back a live specimen of a Troll for the Fitzwilliam Museum. And in due course of time we set out on our quest.

we didn't
bother much about the
Troll just at first.
but after we had
got safely landed
at Esbjaerg
we put our
heads together, & decided to begin our Search
on the Jutland heaths
VJS
J McB
MRJ

Accordingly we started but found

that a days walking over them was very tiring.

moreover there were flies

When we at length reached a barrow, things were much better & we determined to rest till moonrise.

As this spot might be suitable for our researches

We woke suddenly to find that the moon had risen & that a horrible transparent being or Troll was watching us. It was partly like a large bird & partly like a creature with its hands clasped behind it. The apparation remained

absolutely motionless.

We didn't.

The bogs greatly impeded our progress until sunrise, shortly after which we met a native.

He mistook our language & appearance for supernatural on our questioning him, but eventually directed us to a road

which at length led us to Ribe.

After this we were laid up with Colds for some time. but Eventually recovered & went by train to Kolding

When we recovered Sufficiently to bathe with the best of them. and the Danes are keen on bathing.

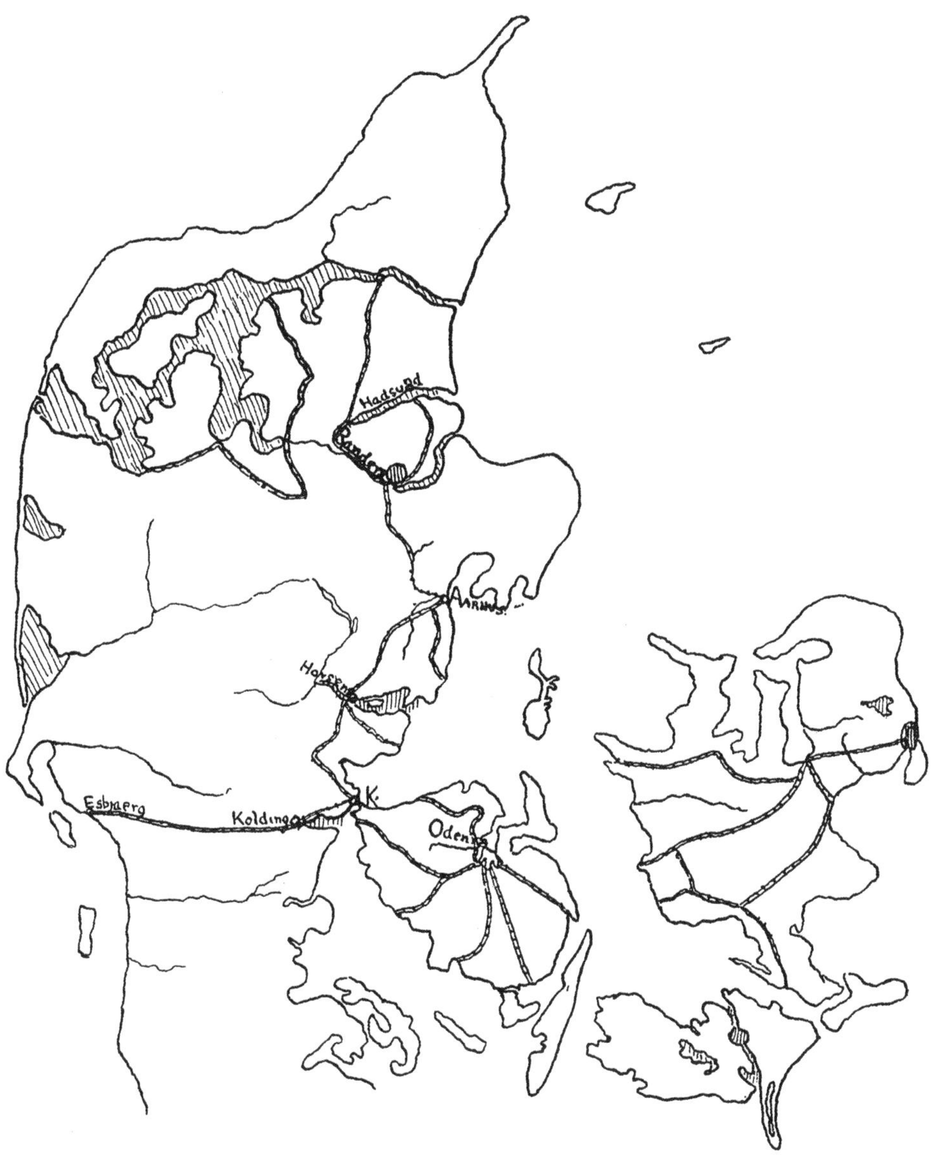

Map of Denmark showing the distribution of Trolls, much used by us at this juncture. (See Baedeker.)

We decided to equip our next expedition more thoughtfully

So one of us went to a bird shop & after some bargaining

bought a large parrot's cage & after a vast amount of preparation we started again in search of Trolls.

This time we were fortunate enough to come upon a small sized Troll asleep

And after a crisp struggle succeeded in overpowering it.

& just before daybreak were able to start for home with our prize in the cage, beginning the journey with such jubilation as our conquest demanded.

But our joy was short lived for we had forgotten

the peculiarities of Trolls & on the first appearance of the sun it burst.

& nothing was left of it but a few grits in our eyes.

we were much dejected when we sat down to breakfast.

The depression consequent upon our want of success lasted for some time. But a bright idea suddenly struck one of us just as he was going to bed.

The more he thought about it the more feasible it appeared.

Accordingly he arose betimes next morning & called the other two.

& forthwith proceeded to disclose his scheme.

& it was agreed unanimously to embark upon it at once.

So having arrived breakfasted one of us set off to the leading wine merchants & purchased considerable quantities of whisky. Whilst another bought supplies from the principal photographers shop.

And we returned with our purchases to the hotel. Even such an ordinary occurrence as this being sufficient to excite the amusement of the natives. Meanwhile the third perused manuscripts in the museum with a view to studying the habits & dates of the Trolls & their assembled allies.

We spent just a day or two speaking Danish to accustom ourselves to conversing freely in that language in case we should find it useful in our encounter with the Trolls

And then confident of success, we set out on our quest for the third time, the inventor of the great scheme leading the way. And as evening came upon us we deposited our skis

and with considerable difficulty succeeded in lighting a camp fire

As we searched about the heath that night we suddenly observed a large assortment of the less responsible Trolls playing leap frog as they advanced from a neighbouring barrow, and knowing from our researches that this was their method of proceeding to their more important assemblies, we lay down till they had passed & then cautiously followed.

We followed these beings across the heath
taking advantage of what cover we could
It was a slow process but after a long pursuit
we arrived at a spot where it was evident
the assembly was taking place

There behind a rock we sat awhile to collect
our thoughts & screw up our courage.
We tossed up who was to peep over the
rock & observe the Trolls.

The observer observing.

What he observed

He was shivering considerably when he returned
we were afraid he had contracted a chill &
gave him some whiskey.

after which he became brighter

so we all took a little

& all became a little brighter.

We started with our stores to the Trolls camp & meant

We discovered carousing. Unfortunately through nervousness the first sip went the wrong way & caused alarming & noisy symptoms

which led to our premature discovery

This was as it happened all for the best as our friend in affliction being scarcely able to see on his recovery & unable to flee, was obliged to explain our sociable & friendly intentions & was bravely stood by him

We placed our whisky at their service & advanced with what Cordiality we were able to assume & were received Courteously by a Troll outpost

who introduced us to a few of his friends. pleasant enough fellows but not good looking.

They took to the whisky with a will and its fame rapidly spread & it soon became obvious that we should have a lively night

We joined in their revels as politeness demanded, but found ourselves
Considerably less Elastic nimble than they were.

3\.
When the night was far advanced we selected a small but healthy troll & craftily mixed the hypo

fixing solution with the drink we gave him. Then at length the whole band fell asleep after their orgy.

We sat & anxiously watched the East grow brighter. But were quite unprepared for the effect of the first glimpse of the Sun.

4. Thanks to his drugged whisky our little troll

Could not burst. And we secured him
& bore him back to the town.

where we rigged him out in a garb calculated
to prevent sunstroke. But we encountered some
difficulty about boots. So we left him

without them. However even when clad like
a mortal the passengers seemed shy of him
just at first when we got him on the steamer for
England.

8.

He broke loose as we started and climbed to the rigging & we were not agile enough to overtake him.

But when the motion began to make itself felt

he became more sort of subdued

& was as quiet & gentlemanly as possible when we landed

He remained so passive on the quay, after the voyage he seemed so docile, that we resolved to take him to the Psychological research dinner in London that evening, & acted accordingly. However, he woke up at the Station

greatly inconvenienced the Company's servants while discharging their duty.

And terrified elderly & respectable gentleman

with his playful ways.

His partiality too for children caused us

considerable uneasiness. Accordingly we had to fasten him with a rope which unfortunately was too long at first & considerable inconvenience was caused by stupid people milk cans which

should get in the way. Luckily he wound himself tightly round a lamp post with his own manouvers: and we were enabled to secure him in a basket & to keep

him there with the help of a friend.

This was given into the Charge of the Guard when the Train arrived.

and freed from responsibility for the present we pursued our journey to Spain in luxury & comfort.

which was not the case with the unfortunate Guard.

Consequently when we reached the Terminus the police interfered. The Doll was sternly ordered to step down.

Which he did.

After this we had ~~the~~ Station & its vicinity to ourselves.
To our relief the Troll was pleased to see
us again, & was much delighted with the proposal
that we should go first to a tailors
to get him a dress suit for the
dinner. We noticed that
the effect of the Potypo was wearing off and
he was becoming more transparent, but
decided to leave him as he was until
the dinner was over. As we
were alone but for the presence
of a
derelict monkey
(which was impudent!) we took the opportunity
of wrapping him in our coats & rugs
So that we could take him through the streets
without exciting
observation.
& Get him
without arousing suspicion into a Hansom Cab.

And all went well until when near our destination, he insisted on looking for the driver

Excited by the success of his observations he insisted further on turning a few back summersaults to the intense alarm of the populace.

Troll for the visitors.

further he boarded a bus which was very disquieting

for the passengers. The most strenuous efforts on the part of the police were insufficient to cope with the agility he displayed, & merely made the force appear ridiculous.

And it was not until he had amused himself in many other ways

that he favoured us with his Company
to proceed to the Tailors. which
fortunately was quite near.
Being the quickest walker he got in first
& gave his order

So we licked the shops up as best we could
& found a suit which met with our
approval, as well as his own.

It was his boots which seemed to cause him most inconvenience when walking to dinner. We had also bought him a wig to improve his appearance but whenever he smiled his mouth always caught in the parting, & we wished him to look pleasant so it had to be discarded. We introduced him to the President who being a psychologist rose to the occasion as heartily as possible. But when dinner began an acute observer might have noticed that the places near the Troll were perhaps less well filled than those at the opposite end of the table. However things went very smoothly till the Troll

was called upon to reply for "The Guests". Which he did.

The Speech was facetious but unfortunately as it was in old Danish no one saw any of the points.

We foresaw trouble;

which came.

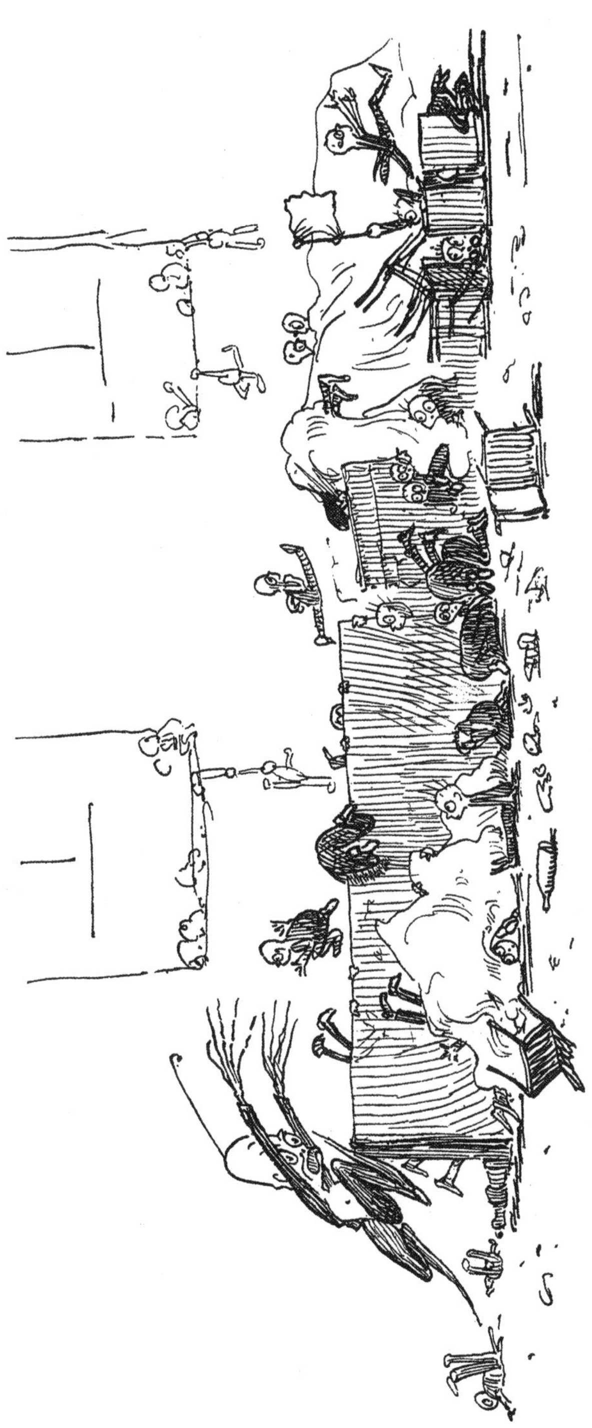

After clearing the room the Troll left the banquet.

with his magnums of champagne. On finding a crowd waiting he cheered up again with the pleasure of being pursued

though sadly hampered by his dress clothes easily distanced his would-be captors

& retired to a prominent position in Trafalgar

Square, whence the united efforts of the police, the fire brigade & the burghers of London failed to dislodge him.

The End

Translation of Script

Because McBryde's whimsical script, with odd spellings and few complete sentences, is sometimes difficult to read, the following (to the best of this reprint editor's ability) is a translation of the text. 100% accuracy is not guaranteed. Questionable words are marked as such.

Page 1:

One evening, while discussing our plans for the Long Vac.*

The idea occurred to us three of making an Expedition to Denmark with the object of bringing back a live specimen of a Troll for the Fitzwilliam museum.** And in due course of time we set out on our quest.

* Vacation.

** The Fitzwilliam Museum at Cambridge University focuses on arts and antiquities.

Page 2:

We didn't bother much about the Troll just at first.

But after we had got safely landed at Ebsjaerg* we put our heads together, and decided to begin our search on the Jutland heaths.

* Should be Esbjerg, a port in Denmark.

Page 3:

Accordingly we started but found that a days walking over there was very tiring.

However there were flies.

When we at length reached a barrow, things were much better and we determined to rest till moonrise.

As the spot might be suitable for our researches.

Page 4:

We woke suddenly to find that the moon had risen and that a horrible transparently benign Troll was watching us. It was partly like a large bird and partly like accusative with its hands clasped behind it.

The apparition remained absolutely motionless.

We didn't.

Page 5:

The bogs greatly impeded our progress until sunrise, shortly after which we met a native.

He mistook our language and appearance for supernatural on our questioning him, but eventually directed us to a road.

Which at length led us to Ribe.*

* Ribe is Denmark's oldest town.

Page 6:

After this we were laid up with colds for some time, but eventually recovered and went by train to Kolding where we recovered sufficiently to bathe with the best of them. And the Danes are keen on bathing.

Page 7:

Map of Denmark showing the distribution of Trolls, much used by us at this juncture.

(See Baedeker.)*

* Baedeker publishes travel guides.

Page 8:

We decided to equip our next expedition more thoughtfully.

So one of us went to a bird shop and after some bargaining bought a large parrot's cage and after a vast amount of preparation we started again in search of Trolls.

Page 9:

This time we were fortunate enough to come upon a small sized Troll asleep and after a crisp struggle succeeded in overpowering it.

And just before daybreak were able to start for home with our prize in the cage, beginning the journey with such jubilation as our conquest demanded.

Page 10:

But our joy was short lived for we had forgotten the peculiarities of Trolls and on the first appearances of the sun it burst.

And nothing was left of it but a few grits in our eyes.

We were much dejected when we sat down to breakfast.

Page 11:

The depression and effects upon our want of success lasted for some time. But a bright idea suddenly struck one of us just as he was going to bed.

The more he thought about it the more feasible it appeared.

Accordingly he arose betimes next morning and called the other two.

And forthwith proceeded to disclose his scheme.

And it was agreed all around to embark upon it at once.

Page 12:

So having armed breakfasted one of us set off to the leading wine merchant and purchased considerable quantities of whisky.

While another bought Hypo* from the principle photographers shop.

And we returned with our purchases to the hotel, even such an ordinary occurrence as this being sufficient to excite the amusement of the inmates [?]. Meanwhile the third perused manuscripts in the museum with a view to studying the habits and dates of assembly of the Trolls and their allies.

* Hypo, or sodium thiosulfate, is a photographic fixing solution.

Page 13:

We spent just a day or two speaking Danish to accustom ourselves to conversing well in that language in case we should find it useful in an encounter with the Trolls.

And then confident of success, we set out on our quest. For the third time, the inventer of the great scheme leading the way. And as evening came upon us we deposited our stores and with considerable difficulty succeeded in lighting a camp fire.

Page 14:

As we searched about the heath that night we suddenly observed a large assortment of the less responsible Trolls playing leap frog as they advanced from a neighbouring barrow, and knowing from our researches that this was their method of proceeding to their more important assemblies, we lay perfectly still, had passed and then cautiously followed.

Page 15:

We followed these beings across the heath taking advantage of what cover we could. It was a slow process but after a long pursuit we arrived at a spot where it was evident the assembly was taking place.

There behind a rock we sat awhile to collect our thoughts and screw up our courage.

We tossed up who was to peep over the rock and observe the Trolls.

The observer observing.

Page 16:

What he observed.

Page 17:

He was shivering considerably when he returned.

We were afraid he had contracted a chill and gave him some whiskey.

After which he became brighter.

So we all took a little.

And all became a little brighter.

Page 18:

We started with ourselves to the Troll's camp and meant to be discovered carousing.

Unfortunately through [?]* that first sip went the wrong way and caused alarming and noisy symptoms.

Which led to our premature discovery.

This was as it happened all for the best as our friend in affliction being scarcely able to see on his recovery and unable to flee, was obliged to explain our sociable and friendly intentions and we bravely stood by him.

* Unknown word.

Page 19:

We placed our whiskey at their service and advanced with what cordiality we were able to assume and were received courteously by a Troll outpost who introduced us to a few of his friends, pleasant enough fellows but not good looking.

They took in the whiskey with a will and its fame rapidly spread and it soon became obvious that we should have a lively night.

Page 20:

We joined in their revels as politeness demanded, but found ourselves considerably less elastic and nimble than they were.

Page 21:

When the night was far advanced we selected a small but healthy troll and craftily mixed the Hypo fixing solution with the drink we gave him.

Then at length the whole band fell asleep after their orgy.

And we sat and anxiously watched the East grow brighter. But were quite unprepared for the effect of the first glimpse of the sun.

Page 22:

Thanks to his drugged whiskey our little troll could not burst. And we secured him and bore him back to the town.

Where we rigged him out in a garb calculated to prevent sunstroke. But we encountered some difficulty about boots. So we left him without them. However even when clad like a mortal the passengers seemed shy of him just at first when we got him on the steamer for England.

Page 23:

He broke loose as we started and took to the rigging and we were not agile enough to overtake him.

But when the motion began to make itself felt
He became more sort of subdued.
And was as quiet and gentlemanly as possible when we landed.

Page 24:

He remained so passively on the queue, after the voyage and seemed so docile, that we resolved to take him to the Psychological research clinic [?] in London that evening, and wired accordingly.

However, he woke up at the station and really inconvenienced the company's servants while discharging their duty.

And terrified elderly and respectable gentlemen with his playful ways.

Page 25:

His partiality too for children caused us considerable uneasiness. Accordingly we had to fasten him with a rope which unfortunately was too long at first and considerable inconvenience was caused by stupid people and milk cans which would get in the way. Luckily he wound himself tightly round a camp post with his own maneuvers; and we were enabled to secure him in a basket and to keep him there with the help of a friend.

Page 26:

This we gave into the charge of the guard when the train arrived.

And freed from responsibility for the present we pursued our journey to train in luxury and comfort.

Which was not the case with the unfortunate guard.

Page 27:

Consequently when we reached the terminus the police interfered. The Troll was sternly ordered to step down.

Which he did.

Page 28:

After this we had the station and its vicinity to ourselves. To our relief the Troll was pleased to see us again, and was much delighted with the proposal that we should go first to a tailor to get him a dress suit for the dinner. We noticed that the effect of the Hypo was wearing off and he was becoming more transparent, but decided to leave him as he was until the dinner was over. As we were alone but for the presence of a derelict monkey (which was impudent), we took the opportunity of wrapping him in overcoats and rugs so that we could take him through the streets without exciting observations and got him without arousing suspicion into a Hansom cab.

Page 29:

And all went well until when near our destination, he insisted on looking for the driver.

Excited by the success of his observations he insisted further on turning a few back summersaults to the intense alarm of the populace.

Troll for the brave. [?]

Page 30:

Further he boarded a bus which was very disquieting for the passengers. The most strenuous efforts on the part of the police were insufficient to cope with the agility he displayed, and merely made the force appear ridiculous.

And it was not until he had amused himself in many other ways

Page 31:

That he favoured us with his company to proceed to the tailors, which fortunately was quite near.

Being the quickest walker he got in first and gave his order.

So we tidied the shop up as best we could and found a suit which met with our approval, as well as his own.

Page 32:

It was his boots which seemed to cause him most inconvenience when walking to dinner.

We had also bought him a wig to improve his appearance but whenever he smiled his mouth always caught in the parting, and we wished him to look pleasant so it had to be discarded.

We introduced him to the president who being a psychologist rose to the occasion as heartily as possible. But when dinner began an acute observer might have noticed that the places near the Troll were perhaps less well filled than those at the opposite end of the table.

However, things went very smoothly till the Troll

Page 33:

Was called upon to reply for "The Guests." Which he did.

The speech was facetious but unfortunately as it was in old Danish no one saw any of his points.

We foresaw trouble; which came.

Page 34:

No Text.

Page 35:

No Text.

Page 36:

After clearing the room the Troll left the banquet with two magnums of champagne. On finding a crowd waiting he cheered up again with the pleasure of being pursued.

And though sadly hampered by his dress clothes easily distanced his would be captors.

Page 37:

And retired to a prominent position in Trafalgar Square, whence the united efforts of the police, the fire brigade and the burghers of London failed to dislodge him.

Page 38:

No Text.

www.ingramcontent.com/pod-product-compliance
Ingram Content Group UK Ltd.
Pitfield, Milton Keynes, MK11 3LW, UK
UKHW061830190726
13855UKWH00005B/1739

9 781930 585256